For Ava: my baby bean, my little 만두, my tiny traveler.
Mommy loves you always and forever. -BBD

For my little adventurers Alexandra and Veronique.
I love you to the moon and back. -SW

Le petit Nomads llc

Written by Brenda Bell Davis
Designed by Brenda Bell Davis and Samantha Wyatt

ISBN: 978-0-9974353-3-7

Approved by the National Media Council UAE. Number 130553

www.LepetitNomads.com

Ava's Adventures Abroad:
Abu Dhabi

Written by Brenda Bell Davis

Designed by Brenda Bell Davis and Samantha Wyatt

This story is not one of your everyday tales.

Listen close, as there are several true and fantastical details.

Once upon a time,

in a land far away,

Lived a little girl named Ava

who went on a trip for a day.

Ava heard tales about flying carpets

and magic lamps in a distant place.

She wanted to travel and see the treasures face-to-face.

So she flew across an ocean

on the back of a great bird.

She landed in the desert,

in the middle of a camel herd.

Ava met a camel named Mike and he gave her a ride.

He volunteered to serve as her treasure-hunting guide.

Mike told Ava that flying carpets and magic lamps

were just stories,

not objects to be found.

Instead, he led her to the land of Abu Dhabi

where riches and real wonders abound.

First, they visited the Sheikh Zayed Grand mosque,

one of the largest in the world.

The mosque had hanging crystals,

a huge carpet,

and the columns were pearled.

Ava and Mike explored the Corniche,

a paved path by the sea.

They viewed fountains and modern buildings;

they even stopped for some tea.

Then they went on a dhow cruise,

and much to their delight...

They glimpsed the Royal Palace,

and pearl filled oysters

oh, what a sight!

Soon after the cruise,

Ava and Mike went on a desert safari in Liwa for two.

They saw a Bedouin village,

a falcon,

and ate Arabian barbecue!

From the top of a tower,

Ava saw the majestic Emirates Palace Hotel.

It was covered in gold and marble,

with rooms for royalty to dwell.

Mike took Ava to Qasr al-Hosn,

the White Fort,

the oldest building about.

It was made of stone,

built to defend,

and keep enemies out!

Next, the two friends set off
to see the wonderful Mangrove National Park.
It was filled with pink flamingos,
dolphins,
and trees with gray bark.

Mike and Ava raced a Saluki

across the famous arched Sheikh Zayed Bridge.

While running along the landmark,

they marveled at its lights and curved ridge.

To conclude the outing,

they went island hopping for fun.

They rode water slides

and drove fast cars on Yas Island,

then relaxed on Saadiyat beach in the sun.

Ava enjoyed her tour in a place of beauty and sand;

Her trip to Abu Dhabi was exceptional,

amazing,

and grand.

Although flying carpets and magic lamps

were not to be found,

Ava knew the riches of Abu Dhabi were all around.

Ava thanked Mike the camel,

gave him a hug,

and told him goodbye.

She departed on the back of the great bird

and flew off into the sky.

CPSIA information can be obtained at www.ICGtesting.com
Printed in the USA
BVIW12n1419061116
467071BV00003B/4